BLADE

IRON ROGUES MC

FIONA DAVENPORT

BLADE

Toby "Blade" Barker didn't plan to claim an old lady like his club president and VP had recently done. As the doctor for the Iron Rogues, his time was rarely his own. But his good intentions went out the window when he met Elise Ayers.

It didn't matter that the injured beauty was too young for him. Or that she was his club brother's little sister. All it took was one look for Blade to know that Elise was meant to be his.

1

ELISE

Working on Christmas wasn't my idea of a good time, but the money was too good to pass up. My brother hadn't been happy about me spending the day at the bar owned by his motorcycle club, the Iron Rogues, but I finally managed to talk him around. I wouldn't have felt comfortable celebrating the holiday at the clubhouse with him and his club brothers because I'd only met a few of them since I came to Tennessee a couple of weeks ago. Plus, I needed the money to help cover my expenses because I wasn't comfortable having Gideon pay for more than my tuition. Something we argued about all the time.

My big brother felt guilty about taking off when he turned eighteen, but I didn't blame him for leaving me behind with our crappy parents. I was just grateful that Gideon had kept in touch over the years, sending money when he could. And that he had stepped in to make sure I could leave for college when I hadn't thought it was possible.

I didn't want to take advantage of him, like our parents had tried when they realized he'd done well for himself. They hated that Gideon had become a biker, but that hadn't stopped them from asking him for money. Which only made me feel worse for accepting his help. The last thing I wanted was for him to think I was anything like them.

Pulling into the parking lot of The Midnight Rebel, I shook off my thoughts about my family and focused on the Christmas song playing over my radio. I'd only worked a handful of shifts at the bar owned by the Iron Rogues and spent yesterday with my brother instead of working, so I wasn't sure what to expect on a holiday. I had assumed it wouldn't be too busy since drinking at a bar wasn't really a Christmassy pastime, but I realized how wrong I was when I had to park all the way in the back of the lot because the place was packed.

Since I had gotten there early, I sat in my car and listened to some more Christmas carols to psych myself up for my shift. I had turned off my headlights and wasn't near a light pole, so it must have seemed as though my vehicle was empty because when I opened my door and climbed out, one of the guys who were standing a couple of spots over from me looked startled by my sudden appearance.

"Shit, man." The tall, thin man facing me dropped a small baggie of white powder on the ground, his hand shaking as he bent over to pick it up.

I gasped as I realized what I had stumbled across —a drug deal.

The dealer glanced over his shoulder to see what had spooked his customer, his beady eyes narrowing and filling with menace when his gaze landed on me. He clenched the cash the other guy had given him in his fist before shoving it into the back pocket of his grungy jeans and muttering, "Don't worry about this. I'll take care of her."

Not liking the sound of that, I swiveled on my foot and jumped back into the driver's seat of my car. And not a moment too soon because as I slammed the door shut, the drug dealer was close enough to pound his fist against the window. "Get outta there, bitch! You're not gonna fuck this up for me!"

No way in heck was I going to step foot out of the car while he was anywhere near, especially when he was screaming at me like that. Jabbing my finger against the ignition button, I thanked my lucky stars that Gideon had insisted on buying me a reliable used car for my high school graduation gift. The engine roared to life, and I quickly put the vehicle into reverse to back out of my parking spot. Slamming his palm against the hood of my car, the dealer yelled for me to stop. That was not going to happen.

Instead, I pressed my foot against the gas pedal while watching in my rearview mirror to make sure I didn't hit anyone as I reversed all the way to the exit of the parking lot. Then I switched into drive as fast as I could and jerked the wheel to turn left onto the street. I wasn't very familiar with Old Bridge, but Gideon had driven me from the clubhouse to the bar on the day I'd gotten the job. Luckily, I was good with directions and remembered the route he had taken.

My hand trembled as I reached over to the passenger seat to pull my cell phone out of my purse. Unfortunately, my distraction cost me because it gave the dealer the chance to catch up to me and slam into the back of my car. My stuff spilled out of my bag and onto the floorboard of the passenger side, making it impossible for me to call Gideon to let him know what was happening.

The Midnight Rebel was only two miles from the Iron Rogues clubhouse, so I stomped my foot against the gas pedal and tried my best to get there before I got hit again. But I only made it a few more blocks before the other vehicle pulled up alongside me and rammed into my door. I gripped the steering wheel as hard as I could, my knuckles turning white, but it didn't do any good.

On the third swipe of the drug dealer's car, I was forced off the road and into the ditch to my right. My airbag went off, protecting my head from hitting the steering wheel, but the contents of my purse that were still on the passenger seat flew up, and something hit my forehead. My engine cut off, and there was a fine dust in the cabin of my car, along with an odd smell in the air.

It took me a moment to shake off my disorientation before I realized the man who had been chasing me was yanking on my door, trying to get it open. If it hadn't been for the roar of a motorcycle driving toward us, he probably would've had enough time to smash in my window and get to me. But when the bike got close enough for the headlight to illuminate the dealer's face, he hissed, "You better keep your mouth shut, bitch. Or else I'm gonna make you pay for fucking with my business."

He slammed his fist against my door before racing back to his car and taking off. I slumped in my seat, taking a few slow breaths to settle my racing heart. But my pulse jumped again when I heard a deep voice call, "Need help?"

Blinking up at the man climbing off his bike, I lifted my hand to my forehead and winced as I brushed my hand against the cut above my brow. My breath caught in my throat when I saw the blood on my fingertips. My eyes widened, and he muttered, "Shit, you're hurt. Can you open the door for me? Gotta check you over to see if you need an ambulance."

Looking through my window, I saw the leather vest he was wearing and heaved a sigh of relief. My rescuer was one of Gideon's club brothers, Whiskey. I knew he couldn't be connected to the guy who'd been chasing me because Gideon had told me that the club refused to have anything to do with drugs.

I reached out to unlock the doors with a slight nod. Opening it, he crouched down next to me.

"Can't believe that bastard had the fucking nerve to hit you and run on our territory." I winced at the fury in his voice, and he shook his head with a grimace. "Sorry, sweetheart. You don't have anything to worry about. I get that you have every right to be scared of being around a big, strange guy after what just happened, but you're safe with me. I swear it."

"I know." I offered him a weak smile. "I'm Elise Ayers, Gideon—um...Storm's—little sister."

His eyes widened. "No shit?"

"Yeah."

"Then I'm doubly glad I was running late to the Christmas bash at the clubhouse." Whiskey undid the buckle on my seat belt and gently lifted it away from my body. "So I was in the right place at the right time to help you. But I shoulda gotten that asshole's plate number. Your brother is gonna want his head for causing your accident and driving away like that."

"It wasn't an accident," I whispered.

His brows drew together as he echoed, "Not an accident?"

"He followed me from The Midnight Rebel," I explained. "I thought if I drove fast enough, I could make it to the clubhouse before he forced me off the road, but he was right behind me. I thought I was going to die, but then you showed up and scared him off. I owe you my life. Thank you."

"Fuck," he bit out, glancing over his shoulder to glare in the direction the drug dealer's car had taken off. Then his concerned gaze returned to scan my face. "Are you hurt anywhere other than the cut on your head? I don't like us being out in the open like this. Want to get you to the clubhouse, where I know you'll be safe."

Getting out of here sounded like the perfect plan to me. "Yeah, I'm good to go."

He helped me out of the car, bending low to sweep my belongings back into my purse and handing it to me before guiding me over to his motor-cycle. "Your car isn't safe to drive so you're gonna have to ride on the back of my bike."

I'd never been on a motorcycle before—Gideon started riding after he left home—so Whiskey had to show me what to do. It was awkward holding a stranger's back while blood dripped down my cheek, but at least the ride was quick, and my brother was walking across the parking lot when we pulled inside the gates.

2

BLADE

"Merry Christmas, Blade!" someone called out. I responded with a half-assed wave and a grunt as I ambled toward one of the long tables set up in the kitchen of the Iron Rogues clubhouse. My prez's old lady had insisted on a party on Christmas Day, and while I would have preferred to be up in my room, passed out in my bed, I didn't want to disappoint Dahlia or piss off Fox by making her unhappy in any way. But after working a double shift in the ER, I was fucking exhausted. Although the delicious smells of the food being prepared made my stomach growl.

The merriment all around me was getting on my nerves, but it wasn't anyone's fault that I was being a grumpy bastard, so I decided to try to avoid further peopling. I fished my phone out of the pocket of my cut and started reading an article about new regenerative medicine technologies.

"You could at least try to have a good time, Blade."

I glanced up to see Sheila, the old lady of one of my club brothers, grinning at me as she approached the table with a large platter of carved turkey. Dropping my phone, I jumped up to grab the serving plate and set it down for her.

"I'm having a good time," I muttered, causing her to laugh and pat my cheek as if I were a child, making me roll my eyes good-naturedly.

Sheila's man, Tank, was one of the oldest active members of the club, having patched long ago when Fox's dad had been president of the MC. She'd been the only old lady for several years—until recently when our prez and VP—Maverick—both fell hard and fast for their women. She was a natural caretaker, so she tended to "mother" us. And we put up with it because, quite frankly, she was awesome, and we all adored her.

"Too bad Santa didn't bring you a woman for Christmas," she teased. "Maybe next year."

"Santa knows better than that," I grumbled.

"Don't have time to deal with female shit. No offense."

Sheila chuckled and winked at me. "None taken. But I'm going to really enjoy seeing some lucky lady knock you on your ass one of these days." With another giggle, she pivoted and headed back to the cooking area for more food.

I followed her to help, and once the tables were loaded down with our dinner, we sat to eat. Before I'd taken more than a few bites, we were startled by the back door banging against the wall as it was shoved open. Storm—our road captain—stumbled in, carrying a woman in his arms. "Blade!" he shouted. "Need your help. Now!"

I jumped up from my spot at the table and rushed over to Storm, taking the shaking woman from him. When my gaze dropped to her pale face, I froze for a second. Shock flooded my system as my heart thumped hard, and my brain screamed, "*Mine!*"

She was fucking breathtaking. Staring up at me with deep brown eyes framed with thick black lashes. Long, dark hair hung in waves, cascading over my arm and down her back. She had mouthwatering curves that felt as if they'd been made just for me, fitting her perfectly in my arms and making me hard as a rock. Her rosebud lips were parted slightly, and she wore a similarly stunned expression. However, something else stood out from my quick perusal. She looked slightly familiar.

Raising my gaze to Storm, I grimaced as I realized that I was most likely holding his little sister. The one he'd warned us all off when he'd asked if she could work at The Midnight Rebel during her winter break from college.

Fucking hell.

"Clinic," I grunted before spinning around and stalking down a hall that led to my medical office. After we entered the building directly behind the clubhouse that housed my clinic, I flipped on the lights before walking straight into the exam room. Reluctant to let her go but knowing I needed to if I wanted to examine her, I set her on the padded table.

"I was in a car accident," she murmured softly. "I got a little lightheaded on the ride here, but I'm fine. Really."

"I'll be the judge of that," I grunted a little more harshly than I'd intended because her sultry voice had sent streaks of desire straight to my dick.

"Watch it," Storm growled, but I ignored him and almost smiled when my girl shot him an annoyed glare. Her face softened when she refocused on me, and I suppressed the desire to gather her up in my arms and kiss the hell out of her.

I started at her hairline since I'd noticed a small cut crusted with blood. "This isn't too deep, but it could use a stitch or two."

"Stitches?" Storm snapped. "What the hell happened, Elise?"

Elise. Damn, her name was as gorgeous as she was.

"Relax, Gideon. I—"

"Relax? Don't tell me to relax, El. One of my brothers just brought my baby sister to me all banged up and needing stitches! I want to know what happened and who the fuck I'm going to kill!" He was bellowing by the time he was done, and Elise winced.

Protective anger surged through me, but I didn't want to make the situation worse, so I dug deep and slipped into professional doctor mode. As much as I could while examining this lush, sexy woman I was determined to keep.

"Storm." My firm, commanding tone caught his attention, and he glared at me. "She most likely has a splitting headache, and you aren't helping her by yelling. Or by stressing her out about what happened. She needs you to be calm right now." Not that I wasn't as determined as my club brother to find out the details, but my first concern was Elise's health.

Storm pressed his lips together, his expression remorseful—but no less determined—as he crossed his arms over his chest, then nodded.

A small bruise was forming on her jaw, and I had to fight back the impulse to kiss it, along with any other injuries I encountered. Instead, I focused on her mouth, but then I couldn't stop thinking about those pouty lips wrapped around my cock.

Shaking my head to dispel the thoughts, I again attempted to put on my doctor's hat and treat her like any other patient. But it didn't work very well, and as I proceeded to do a thorough check of her body, it was like fucking torture since every inch of her was soft and supple. When I placed a blood pressure cuff on her arm, it felt toned, and I imagined that her grip when she wrapped her hand around my dick would be strong. Her large tits quivered when I pulled aside the neck of her T-shirt to place my stethoscope on her silky skin. I had to fight back a groan when my hands brushed the undersides of her breasts as I felt for broken ribs.

I gently checked her legs for broken bones and found them also surprisingly toned for being so deliciously curvy. I couldn't wait to feel them squeezing my waist while I was buried deep inside her.

Pathetic, Dr. Barker, I admonished myself. *She's your patient.* But really, she was so much more than that. I was simply the only one who knew it at the moment.

Finally, I finished and breathed a sigh of relief, though I was loath to stop touching her. If I didn't, I would eventually snap, and it wasn't the time or place to lose my control with Elise.

"Good news is that your injuries are minor," I told her with a smile. "Ankle is bruised. Not sprained or broken. Bad news is that you will likely be pretty sore tomorrow. Gonna stitch that cut and wrap your ankle. I'll give you a couple of mild painkillers to help soothe your aches. A hot bath would also help."

Hell. Now I was picturing her wet and naked with suds gliding down her milky skin...

A knock sounded on the door, pulling me away from the images that would haunt me until I could see the real thing.

"Everybody decent?" Whiskey called from the other side.

"Yeah," Storm grunted as he twisted the knob to open the door and let our sergeant at arms into the room.

All eyes went to Whiskey, but he was staring at Elise, his head cocked to the side.

"I just wanted to check on you. How're you doin'?"

His eyes held nothing but concern, but jealousy slithered through my veins for some reason, and my stomach soured.

Elise smiled, and I wanted to growl and demand that she only ever smile at me. But that would make me sound like a fucking lunatic, so I gritted my teeth and kept my mouth shut.

"I'm good. Thank you so much again for rescuing me. It would have taken me hours to limp my way here if I'd even gotten the chance."

The idea of her alone, out in the dark, cold and injured, making her way here... made me want to put my fist through a wall. But the realization that Elise had arrived here on the back of Whiskey's bike was almost as rage-inducing.

"No problem," Whiskey said gruffly. "Glad you're okay. You need anything—"

"She'll come to me," I snapped, cutting him off.

Whiskey and Storm looked at me in surprise, but while Whiskey's expression turned amused, Storm's eyes narrowed in suspicion.

I thought about clarifying that I meant she could

come to me as a doctor, but what the hell. It would be very clear, sooner rather than later, that Elise belonged to me.

"Understood," Whiskey murmured before raising his chin in farewell and leaving.

Storm had been leaning against the wall, but he shoved his body away from it and stalked over to stand beside his sister. "Off-limits, Blade," he gritted through clenched teeth. "Stay the hell away from my sister."

3

ELISE

"Pardon me?" I huffed, crossing my arms against my chest. "Did you seriously just warn your friend off me? As though you have any say in who I may or may not want to date?"

Gideon thrust his chin out. "Damn straight, I did. And I do."

Planting my fists on my hips, I glared up at him. "Just because you're covering the rest of my tuition doesn't make you the boss of me."

"Maybe not," he conceded. "But being your big brother does."

I shook my head. "Nope."

"Yup."

"Nuh-uh."

"Uh-huh."

Rolling my eyes, I sighed. "What are you, twelve?"

He quirked a brow and chuckled. "What are you, a teenager?"

"Yes, but barely, which you very well know," I huffed.

The sexy biker who'd examined me leaned his hip against the counter lining the wall opposite the exam table I sat on, his gaze darting between us as my brother and I bickered like we were little kids. The ten years between us didn't stop the normal rivalry between siblings. Gideon was a great big brother, but that never stopped me from pushing his buttons. And he'd never had a problem with poking me right back, even when I was a toddler.

Acutely aware of the man who seemed to be enjoying the show Gideon and I were putting on, I decided to end it. The last thing I needed was for the first guy to spark my libido to see me as a little kid because I tended to act like one when I was around my brother.

"But seriously, I've been on my own for years with very little supervision from our parents. I've practically raised myself ever since you left home. You weren't around to complain about any boys I might've dated up until now, so I find it incredibly hypocritical of you to think you have a say now."

Blade's eyes narrowed toward the end of my tirade, and I briefly wondered if he wasn't happy about me mentioning my dating life. My nonexistent one since there hadn't been time for me to worry about boys when I was studying my butt off to make sure my grades were good enough to get into college with a decent scholarship while also working part-time so I'd have some cash to help pay for living expenses while I was at school. Not to mention that I hadn't met a guy tempting enough to sway me from my goals.

Until now.

With his light brown hair and intense gray eyes, Blade was beyond handsome. Add in the scruff on his cheeks, his tall, muscular body, and his dangerous air, and you had an irresistible combination that had my panties almost spontaneously combusting each time he'd put his hands on me during his examination.

I'd never felt anything like my reaction to him, which only made my brother's warning even more frustrating.

"No interfering with my dating life."

"Fine," Gideon conceded. "I'll back off for now,

but I still reserve the right to kick anyone's ass who hurts you."

"Nah, I'll do it myself, using the skills you made sure I had." I crossed my ankles, barely holding back a wince at the twinge of pain that shot up my leg. "You know that I kept up with those self-defense lessons because you're the one who paid for them."

"You heard your sister. She can take care of herself." Blade flashed my brother a smug grin, and I returned my attention to the hot biker who'd examined me.

I turned my ire on him. "Don't think you're getting off scot-free. I saw that look you aimed at Whiskey. It was completely uncalled for, especially since I owe him my life."

Gideon's head tilted to the side as he echoed, "Saved your life? Don't you think you're laying it on a little thick there, sis? Blade just said your injuries from the car accident weren't that bad."

"Because they're not." The Iron Rogues doctor's eyes narrowed. "Definitely nowhere near life-threatening, or we wouldn't be sitting here talking like this. I'd have already hauled her ass to the hospital to make sure she survived."

"Then why the hell are you talking like Whiskey

rode in like your white knight to save you when you were just in a car accident, El?" Gideon asked.

"It wasn't just a car accident," I corrected, shaking my head as I rubbed my palms up and down my arms. "I saw something that I shouldn't have and was followed from the bar on my way to get to you."

"Shit." Gideon raked his fingers through his hair. "I was so rattled by you getting hurt that I didn't even stop to think about why you weren't pulling your shift at Midnight Rebel. What the fuck happened?"

"Since you had already left for the clubhouse, I decided to head to the bar early for my shift."

"Why the fuck is your sister working in one of our bars instead of celebrating the holiday with the club?" Blade growled, glaring at my brother. "None of this would've happened if she'd been here with us, where she belongs."

"You think I don't know that?" Gideon hissed. "I'm already kicking my own ass for not putting my foot down about that damn job. I don't need you to do it, too. Not when you have zero say in my sister's life."

I pinched the bridge of my nose between my thumb and index finger. "Are you guys going to keep bickering over something neither of you get to decide? Or are we going to focus on the actual problem so you can find the guy who tried to kill me?"

"Tried to kill you?" they echoed together at the top of their lungs.

"That's what I'm trying to explain." I dropped my hand to my side. "I wasn't paying as much attention to my surroundings as I should have while I listened to Christmas music before going inside. So I didn't realize what was happening a couple of parking spots over until I got out of my car."

"I've told you over and over again how important situational awareness is, Elise. You're a nineteen-year-old girl, and most guys have a good fifty pounds and half a foot on you. You've gotta pay attention to your surroundings so you can stay safe. No matter how many self-defense lessons you've taken, your best bet is to avoid the fight in the first place."

"Yeah, well, that's hard to do when there's a drug deal going down in a parking lot where I thought I'd be safe because it's owned by the Iron Rogues." I hopped off the exam table to pace—gingerly, since my ankle was still a little sore—back and forth in front of the two men who were finally focused on me. "You told me that I didn't have to worry about stuff like that while I was working there, but the second I climbed out of my car, I saw a guy handing over a bag of what I'm guessing was cocaine to another guy who looked as though he was strung out."

"What'd they look like?" Blade demanded.

I gave them all the details I could remember about the drug dealer and his customer, as well as the car that had chased me.

Gideon clenched his fists at his sides. "That motherfucker forced you off the road?"

I nodded. "Yeah, and then he tried to force his way into my car. I'm not sure what he had planned from there, except that it wasn't going to be good for me. He was pissed that I stumbled across his drug deal and was yelling about how he wasn't going to let me...um...mess things up for him. If Whiskey hadn't shown up when he did, I don't think I would've gotten away from him."

"Everyone knows we don't allow drugs in our territory." My brother looked at Blade. "The punishment he faced for getting caught dealing at one of our bars would've been severe."

"And he made it a whole hell of a lot worse for going after her," Blade growled.

Butterflies swirled in my belly over how angry the sexy doctor seemed to be on my behalf. "He had no way of knowing who I was, though. He probably figured I was just some server who the club would be pissed at for missing her shift."

"Then he's even dumber than we already thought." At my look of confusion, Gideon explained, "The guy already proved to be a fucking idiot for blatantly breaking one of our rules out in the open where he was practically begging to be caught. But he should've known that the people who work for us are under our protection."

Blade nodded in agreement, a determined gleam in his gray eyes. "He's gonna pay. The statement will be made—nobody hurts you. Ever."

4

BLADE

After I'd stitched and bandaged up Elise, Storm held out his hand and helped his sister off the exam table. I wanted to snatch her hand away and tuck her into my side. Since I knew staking my claim on her right then would lead to a fight—probably a very violent one—with Storm, and I didn't want to ruin everyone's Christmas, I stepped back and let him lead his sister back to the clubhouse and into the kitchen.

People were picking at their food, but by how they all perked up when we walked into the room, they'd been more interested in learning what had happened.

Storm took Elise to the table where Fox, Mav, and their women sat. "Need to talk," he told the men gruffly. Sensing his urgency, especially when they saw my expression as well, they nodded and climbed to their feet.

Fox's gaze shifted to Elise, then back to me, rather than Storm. Not much got past our prez, which was how he'd earned his road name. "Molly and Dahlia will take care of her," he assured me, though Storm was the one who responded.

"Thanks." His face softened when his eyes went to his sister. "You'll be okay?"

"You're, um...all going?" she asked.

"I won't be long," Storm assured her, putting his arm around her for a quick hug that made me want to rip the limb clean off.

"Okay." Elise's brown eyes darted in my direction for just a moment, but it was long enough for me to see a spark of disappointment. I suppressed a smile as I followed my brothers to the door. Before I left, I glanced back and winked at her. Twin spots of pink bloomed on her cheeks, and her plush mouth rose slightly at the corners.

As I made my way to the prez's office, I wondered how much of that pretty blush would cover her body when I made her come. "Dammit," I grunted, trying to think of something that would get rid of the steel shaft in my pants. Carefully, since I was painfully hard, I adjusted myself before entering the office.

I quickly dropped onto a chair and silently exhaled in relief when no one seemed to notice the state of my groin.

Before anyone could speak, Whiskey joined us, followed by a few enforcers—including Deviant, who was our tech expert. I felt an irrational surge of aggression toward Whiskey, but I couldn't help it. Especially anytime I thought about my woman on the back of his bike. As grateful as I was to him for showing up in time to save Elise from that bastard, I hated the idea of her wrapped around him.

I was incredibly relieved when Fox started the meeting because it took my mind off all the ways I wanted to kick Whiskey's ass. And my fury at Elise's attacker eclipsed my growing hunger for her.

"What happened?" Fox asked Storm.

Elise's brother explained the situation, and as he told them about the drug deal she'd witnessed, the tension in the room became deadly.

The Iron Rogues often worked outside the law, and we had our own brand of justice. Our hands were all kinds of dirty, but we didn't tolerate any association with drugs. Any members caught using were given the choice of rehab or leaving the MC—the first time.

We didn't allow them in our businesses, and we'd even assisted local law enforcement in busting up some drug rings in the area...unofficially.

Our zero tolerance for drugs was no secret, so finding out that this lowlife had not only violated our rules but then attempted to kill an innocent woman to avoid being caught had every one of us itching to put a bullet in the asshole. Especially since she belonged to the club—first as Storm's sister and now because she would be my old lady.

Fox's dark gaze landed on Deviant. "Have Savage send over the security footage. Do whatever you have to. Get me a motherfucking name."

After Deviant nodded, Storm spoke up. "I can comb the security footage—"

Fox held up his hand, making Storm go silent. "You have to leave on a run tomorrow."

Storm blinked, then his expression filled with guilt. "Right. Shit. Can't believe I forgot." A tortured look entered his eyes, and he ran his hands through his hair. "But my sister—"

"She's got all of us, brother," Mav assured him. "You know every one of us will protect her with our

life. And we'll let you know as soon as we have something to go on."

"I'll come right back."

Fox shook his head. "No. Focus on the run and
on your woman. If shit hasn't been handled when
you get back, we'll get you up to speed and let you
handle the asshole. Blakely comes first. You've
waited long enough, and that situation could blow
the fuck up any day."

I understood why Storm was torn. He felt like he
was choosing between his sister and his woman. Not
that he'd claimed her since she'd just barely turned
eighteen a week ago. She wasn't living in great
circumstances, and he wanted to get her out before
anything damaging happened.

My instinct was to tell him that I would take care
of Elise myself, that she was mine and I'd never let
anything happen to her. But I had a feeling that
would only make matters worse. His head was a mess
right then, and he needed to clear it and focus. So I
made the vow silently, if only to make myself feel
better.

We strategized for another ten minutes, then
agreed to meet again the next day after Storm and
the others accompanying him had left. It was still
Christmas, and a party was in full swing. The last

thing any of us wanted was to ruin anything and make Molly or Dahlia cry—which they did way too fucking often since they'd been knocked up.

When we returned to the kitchen—with the exception of Deviant, who'd chosen to get right to work—everyone was eating, and the mood was light.

My gaze immediately found Elise, and my lips curved up when I saw her talking to Molly with a beautiful smile. Dahlia was on the other side of Elise, and she leaned in to say something, making all three women burst into laughter.

Seeing as how I'd made up my mind to keep Elise, I was happy that she seemed so comfortable with the other old ladies. It would make her transition much easier. Although after hearing her comments to Storm about his absence in her life, I realized she wasn't as familiar with our lifestyle as I'd first assumed. Some women struggled with the concept of the MC being a brotherhood and the lines drawn between them and the club business. However, some MCs, like the Iron Rogues and the Silver Saints, made sure our women knew our commitment to them was every bit as strong as our loyalty to our brothers. The only secrets I would ever keep from Elise would involve club business, and considering the nature of it, I wouldn't want it touching her anyway.

I took a step toward her table, but halted when Storm took the chair directly across from his sister. The last thing I wanted to do was drive a wedge between the siblings or cause a fight on Christmas. Fighting my instincts and desire to be near her, I went back to my original seat.

From my vantage point, I had a clear view of Elise, and I couldn't drag my eyes away from her. After a few grunted responses, my tablemates stopped trying to engage me in conversation, leaving me to eat and brood in relative peace.

Several times throughout the evening, Elise glanced my way, and when our eyes met, I didn't bother to hide the heat in mine. Sometimes, she would shiver, making me grin and causing her to blush before she turned her attention away.

It was hard as fuck not to grab her and make a run for it, but I kept myself in check with the reminder that Storm would be leaving the next day. I'd have time without his interference to convince Elise that she was meant to be mine.

Once we took care of the son of a bitch who'd nearly killed her, we'd work out the details for the future. I knew she was in school, but not locally, so we'd have to change that ASAP since I couldn't protect her if she wasn't with me. And I didn't intend to sleep without her after tonight. I didn't want to wait to start our life together.

I probably shouldn't have been surprised by the sudden desire to see her big and round with my kid growing inside her. But I was still reeling a little from falling head over heels for her in an instant. However, it all felt incredibly right, so I hadn't questioned my reaction to Elise. Besides, I'd seen it happen with Fox and Maverick. The moment we met, Elise became my future. My forever.

5

ELISE

My Christmas hadn't gone anything like I had expected. Instead of earning some extra cash, I'd almost been killed, and now my brother was insisting that I couldn't go back to work because it wasn't safe for me to be there anymore. And it didn't matter how much I argued since his club president had backed him up. My job was gone, and I'd barely padded my bank account since I'd come to Old Bridge.

Rolling over in my bed, I buried my face in my pillow with a groan. My body was achy from the crash, and my head throbbed a little where Blade had stitched up my cut. Today wasn't getting off to a great start, that was for sure. And it only got worse when my brother stopped me from falling back asleep.

"Pack up your stuff, El." Gideon rapped his knuckles against the connecting door between our motel rooms. "It's time to go."

Sliding off the mattress, I stomped across the room and flung the door open. "Go where?"

"To the clubhouse." He flung his duffel bag over his shoulder and jerked his chin toward my room. "Don't take too long. I need to be there in twenty minutes."

My brows drew together. "Why do I need to pack to go to the clubhouse?"

"Because you're gonna stay there while I'm gone."

"Gone?" I echoed softly, leaning against the doorframe while I stared up at him. "Where are you going? And I thought you didn't want me staying at the clubhouse? Isn't that why you booked us into the motel while I'm here? Because it wouldn't be appropriate for me to be there without you."

"I didn't word it quite like that," he grumbled, dropping his bag at my feet to shove his way past me and sit down on the chair in the corner of my room. Propping his feet up on the ottoman, he ignored my glare while he got comfortable. "It's just that I didn't want any of the guys to get the wrong idea about you hanging around the clubhouse."

Flopping onto the corner of the mattress, I huffed, "I still don't understand the problem. I thought you said I didn't have to worry about stuff like club whores with the Iron Rogues."

"Fucking A, El," he groaned, shaking his head. "Club whores? You can't say shit like that."

I shrugged, flashing him a mischievous smile. "Sorry, but that's what they call them on television. Should I have said club bunnies instead? Sweet butts? House mouses? Or would that be mice? I'm not sure what the plural would be when you're talking about women instead of rodents."

He grimaced, his eyes narrowing. "What kind of shit have you been watching?"

"Whatever I wanted," I retorted with a smug grin. "It's not as though Mom and Dad paid attention to anything I did."

"Wish I could say I'm surprised, but I'm not." He looked pained at the reminder of my crappy childhood, which made me feel bad for bringing it up again. "I'm so damn sorry."

Getting to my feet, I padded over to pat his hand. "You don't need to apologize for our crappy parents. You had it just as bad with them as I did."

"Yeah, but that's why I should've done a better job of protecting you from them." He flipped his hand over to squeeze mine. "Because I know just how detached they were with me."

"As far as I'm concerned, you have nothing to apologize for. And they can be as hands-off as they'd like now because I have no intention of staying in contact with them. Not that they'll even notice since they didn't have a peep to say about me not showing up for Christmas break." Not wanting to talk—or think—about our parents anymore, I changed the subject. "You still haven't answered my original question. Where are you going?"

"Out of town for a few days. Maybe a week." He heaved a deep sigh, his eyes filled with regret. "I can't give you too many details, club business."

I'd seen enough motorcycle club shows to know that meant I wasn't going to get any more information out of him. "And you want me to stay at the clubhouse. By myself? For however long you're gone?"

"No, I need you to stay there so I'll know you're safe. Or else, I'm gonna worry about you the whole time, and that'll be bad for me."

I didn't know what Gideon would be doing for the club, but I didn't want to risk himself because he was scared something would happen to me. "Then I guess I'd better go pack so we can hit the road, or else you'll be late."

"That'd be great, Els." He beamed me a grateful smile and got to his feet. "And don't worry, Tank told me that Sheila said she would make sure my room was clean before we got there, so you won't have to deal with my mess while you stay there."

Just thinking about the kind of things I would've found in there—or on the sheets—made me gag. Shooing him out of my room as he chuckled over my reaction, I headed into the bathroom to get cleaned up and changed into my favorite pair of jeans and a cute sweater. Then I quickly shoved my stuff into my bag so we could check out of our rooms early. Since the club owned the motel, we didn't run into any issues and were on our way to the clubhouse in the truck he rarely drove only fifteen minutes later.

After we dropped my stuff off in his room—which was thankfully clean as promised—we headed down to the kitchen. Sheila stood at the stove, so I hurried over to her. "Thank you so much for making sure I didn't need a hazmat suit."

"No worries," she assured me with a soft laugh. "I was happy to help."

"It was very much appreciated." Breathing in the

delicious aroma from the pan in front of her, I added, "And so would a few pieces of bacon. We didn't have time for breakfast since my brother was in a rush to get here."

"Have as much as you'd like," she offered, plopping several strips onto the paper-towel lined plate stacked high with bacon. "I always make plenty since the guys put away food as if they think it will be their last meal."

"Thanks." I snagged a piece and munched on it until Gideon pulled me to the side for a hug.

"Promise me you'll listen to what my club brothers tell you to do while I'm gone," he requested. "They'll keep you safe since I can't be here to keep an eye on you."

Remembering the close call I'd had the night before sent a shiver of dread up my spine. "You don't have to worry about me, Gideon. I'm not going to do anything to risk myself. I promise."

"This is shit timing." A muscle jumped in his jaw. "I hate leaving you like this. We hardly get any time together as it is, and the crap you went through last night just makes it worse. If I was leaving for any other reason, I'd ask one of the guys to cover for me, but it just isn't possible."

"I'm fine, I swear." I beamed a smile up at him. "I

only got a little bruised up, remember? Blade said so himself."

"What'd I say?" the biker who sent my pulse into overdrive asked as he strode into the kitchen, catching the tail end of what I was saying to my brother.

"That I'm fine."

"Too damn true." His heated gaze swept down the length of my body, leaving goose bumps in its wake because it felt as though he was actually touching me.

My brother elbowed him in the side. "Medically, asshat."

Viper, one of the other club brothers who I'd briefly met yesterday, popped his head in the kitchen door and called, "Time to go, Storm."

"Remember your promise, El." My brother gave me a quick hug. "Stay safe while I'm gone."

It felt weird saying goodbye to Gideon, knowing I would be staying at the Iron Rogues clubhouse without him after he'd made such a big deal about us staying at the motel when I got into town. But I couldn't let him see my discomfort, so I beamed a smile at him. "Will do."

He pointed at Blade. "Protect her."

"With my life if it comes down to it." The weight

in Blade's vow made me a little weak in the knees, but he must've noticed because he wrapped his arm around my waist as Gideon strode out of the kitchen. "Don't worry, baby. I won't let anything happen to you."

"I know it'll sound weird, but even after what happened last night, I'm not worried about myself." I leaned against his side. "My brother wouldn't have left me with you guys if he wasn't certain you'd find the drug dealer before he can get to me. But I can't shake the feeling that he's the one in actual danger."

"Can't share club business with you, but I can say that Storm will have Viper at his back while he's gone. He'll be fine."

"He better be," I muttered just as my stomach let out a loud rumble.

"Sounds as though you need some breakfast." Blade dropped his hand to my lower back to guide me over to the counter where Sheila had laid out all the food. Everything looked too good to pass up, so I decided to eat my worries away.

6

BLADE

The rational side of my brain was telling me to take things slow with Elise. She was young—too damn young for me, but that wasn't going to stop me from claiming her—and we'd met less than twenty-four hours ago.

But the other part was dying to be inside her, and now that her brother wasn't an obstacle...

It was a fight in my head, but after watching Elise eat...seeing her moan with delight and slide her fork in and out of her plush, fuckable lips...the need to fuck her won out.

By the time she finished, I was surprised that my dick hadn't punched through my pants. I was a big guy, and my long, thick cock was hard as hell, pressing tight against the zipper, which was probably leaving teeth marks in the sensitive skin.

Biting back a groan of pain, I stood from the table and took our dishes to the sink. When I turned and headed back to my girl, I saw Molly sit down next to her and begin to say something.

"Why don't you come to our house while Storm is gone? No one here would hurt you, but since you aren't claimed, you'll probably get really sick of every guy around hitting on you."

Molly giggled at her words, but they ignited a fire in my belly. She was wrong. Elise was taken, and I was gonna make sure everyone knew it. Starting with her.

"She's staying with me," I grunted in a tone that made it clear this wasn't up for discussion.

Molly raised an eyebrow, but her green orbs were twinkling with amusement. However, it was Elise's reaction that I paid attention to.

She turned in her seat and looked up at me, then double-blinked, her mouth parting in surprise. After a few seconds, she sighed. "You don't have to watch over me just because I'm Storm's sister. I—"

"Don't give a fuck about your brother," I growled as I came to stand directly in front of her and held out my hand. "You're m—staying with me." I'd almost declared that she belonged to me, but I caught myself at the last second because I didn't want to have that discussion until we were alone in my room.

Elise's lips curled up, and her brown eyes sparked with excitement as she placed her palm in mine. "Okay," she agreed softly.

I helped her to her feet and lifted my chin at Molly, ignoring her knowing smirk, then led Elise out of the kitchen. While I had an apartment not far from the compound, I kept a permanent room in the clubhouse because I often needed to be here for someone overnight or to just crash if I treated someone at odd hours. I would have preferred to take Elise to my place, but I didn't want her leaving the compound until the asshole who tried to kill her had been dealt with.

Deviant had discovered the guy's name, but he hadn't been able to locate him so far. All of our businesses were on the MC owned land in the town surrounding the compound, and most of the apartment buildings and houses were with either patches, prospects, or loyal families, so it was unlikely that he was local. What we were most concerned about was whether this was a one-time deal, or if the scumbag was part of a bigger drug ring that had decided to encroach on our territory.

I planned to jump into helping out with the investigation tomorrow, but for tonight, I was going to put all my focus on my woman.

My room was on the first floor, at the back of the house so that it was nearest to the clinic. There were a few suite-type rooms down that hall, but they were mostly used whenever one of my club brothers who didn't have their own space needed to crash at the last minute or for guests. So it was pretty isolated, and that suited me just fine since I wasn't keen on the idea of anyone hearing Elise screaming my name. Although, it was certainly one way to stake my claim.

When we reached our destination, I fished a key out of my pocket and unlocked the door before shoving it open and gesturing for her to enter. Being a doctor, I was used to keeping things organized and tidy. So the king bed was made and the only clutter was a worn paperback on one of the oak nightstands and a few items I'd left on the long dresser that faced the bed with a large flatscreen mounted above it.

The exterior wall had two windows, and beneath one of them was an old, comfy leather chair with a small table next to it. Elise wandered over and sat down, then turned on the little lamp and picked up the framed photo I kept there.

Her forehead puckered as she gazed at the two

laughing toddlers in the picture. "You're a dad?" Her eyes met mine, filled with confusion and hesitance.

"That's my niece, Darrah, and my nephew, Devon," I explained. Relief flooded her features, and I cocked my head to the side, studying her. "Do you want kids?"

A bright smile instantly spread across her face, giving me my answer before she said a word. "Oh, yes. I want lots of them." She traced the cherub faces in the photo and sighed. "I love my brother to pieces, and he did his best to be there for me, but for the most part, I grew up like an only child since there are ten years between us. My parents were rarely there, and when they were, they acted like I wasn't. I don't want my kids to ever feel that kind of loneliness."

I was happy to hear that she wanted a big family, but my chest ached at the sadness and pain she'd endured. Her parents were definitely on my shit list, and they had better stay the hell away from my woman.

"I wouldn't mind if you already had kids," she added with a soft smile. "I just don't want to be a wedge that breaks a family apart."

It baffled me that someone who'd been basically abandoned by her family—even by Storm to a certain extent—had such compassion. Just from watching her last night and today, it was already clear that she had a huge heart and a great capacity for love.

Hopefully, it wouldn't be long before her heart belonged to me. But I was gonna start with her body. The sexual tension had been building since I'd shut and locked the door behind us, despite the serious conversation.

Elise's pale skin was tinged with pink, and when I raked my heated eyes over her, I noticed her peaked nipples poking through her thin sweater. Her flushed skin darkened when I prowled over to stand in front of her. She was eye level with my groin, and when her gaze dropped to the bulge there, her eyes widened before whipping back up to meet my gaze. Her tongue darted out to wet her bottom lip, leaving it shiny and so very tempting.

A deep groan rumbled in my chest as I grabbed her hands and yanked her to her feet. I locked them around my neck, then splayed mine on her back, plastering her body against my chest as my mouth crashed down onto hers.

She tasted sweet and warm, like apple pie straight from the oven. It made me ravenous, and I devoured her while my hands glided around her rib cage and under her sweater to cup her big, soft tits. They more than filled my hands, and the soft little whimper she made when I squeezed them had come oozing from my dick.

Slowly, I dragged my mouth down to her jaw and placed hot, wet kisses on her neck, sucking here and there to leave my mark. Elise dropped her head back and tunneled her hands into my hair.

When I released her breasts, she whimpered in protest, making me chuckle. "Patience, baby." Then I grabbed the hem of her sweater and whipped it up over her head. She was practically spilling out of her lacy, black bra, and I licked my lips as I yanked down the cups and bent to suck one rosy peak into my mouth.

"Blade," she gasped as she arched her back.

I let her nipple go with a pop and looked straight into her eyes when I firmly squeezed her generous globes and growled, "Toby. You call me Toby, Elise."

Her brown eyes practically melted into chocolate, and she nodded with a sweet smile. "Toby."

"Fuck," I grunted, closing my eyes and trying to quell the rush of pleasure that was threatening to make me come in my pants like a horny teenager. "Hearing you say my name in that sexy voice...damn, baby. It's hot as fuck." I latched onto her nipple again, sucking and nibbling while my fingers twisted and plucked at the other one. Then I switched and did the same to the opposite side.

My mouth returned to hers, and I palmed her ass, dragging her up against me, lifting her off her toes so that the bulge in my pants was cradled in the apex of her thighs.

I could feel her heat and couldn't stand the barriers between us any longer. Tearing my mouth away, I drank in the sight of her tits bouncing with her choppy breaths while I unhooked her bra. I didn't wait for her to shrug it off before attacking the button on her jeans and yanking them down her legs.

My mouth watered at the sight of her curvy hips and thick thighs. She had on matching underwear, and I rubbed my nose over the damp lace as I inhaled deeply. "You smell like heaven," I rasped. "Can't wait to taste."

Elise gasped, and I grinned wickedly up at her astonished expression. "You want to—oh!"

I fisted the fabric at the center of her panties and ripped them away, then immediately dragged my tongue up her slit. "Holy shit, baby," I moaned. "Even better than I imagined."

Her legs quivered, and she latched onto my shoulders to steady herself.

I wanted to savor every lick of her sweet, juicy

pussy, but I was already hanging by a thread, I needed to be inside her. So I didn't waste any time, eating her to her peak and using a finger to push her into a hard, fast climax.

"Oh, yes! Toby!" Elise screamed as her body shook and her pussy spasmed around my digit.

I shot to my feet and swept her up into my arms, then gently laid her on the bed. She was still in a state of blissful oblivion when I shucked my clothes and covered her body with mine. She was tiny compared to me, and it made me feel even more protective and possessive of her.

"Fuck, baby. You feel so good under me." Her hot skin was damp, and it practically burned wherever we touched. I was leaking a steady stream of come from the fat, swollen head of my cock, so I slid easily between her folds. She cried out when I rubbed against her clit. "So wet," I groaned. "Need in you."

"Yes," she hissed, clutching my sides so hard her nails dug into my flesh.

The small bite of pain sent streaks of pleasure through me, and I notched the head of my cock at her entrance. A small bubble of sanity broke through my haze, and I paused, realizing that I'd almost plowed right into her without knowing if I needed to be careful.

She was tiny, so it was bound to be a very tight fit. And if she was untouched...the thought sent another spurt of come out of my dick, making her entrance slick, which was good since it would help me slide in easier.

"Elise, baby," I rumbled in a low, gritty voice. "Are you a virgin?"

She froze for a second, then her gaze dropped to my chest, and she nodded.

I squeezed my eyes shut, trying to gain more control now that I knew I would be the first and only cock to ever feel the grip of her hot little pussy.

When I opened them, she was still staring at my chest and her cheeks were burning with a crimson blush.

"Elise, look at me," I demanded.

Slowly, she lifted her gaze to my face, and relief sparked in her brown orbs when she saw my smile.

"It wouldn't matter to me if I wasn't your first, but the possessive asshole inside me is fucking ecstatic that I'm the only man who will ever know what it's like to be inside you."

Her face flushed with pleasure this time, and I sealed my words with a long, deep kiss. When I retreated, I gazed down at her, smiling smugly at the dazed expression on her beautiful face. I bent my head so that my lips brushed her ear when I asked, "Are you on birth control, baby?"

She shivered and moaned, "Um...no...I...what— oh, my gosh! Oh, yesss."

I hadn't given her any time to really think about the situation once I had my answer. I pushed into her channel, a little at a time, giving her muscles a chance to stretch to accommodate my giant cock. When I felt her hymen, I paused and stared down into her deep, brown pools. "Gonna be very clear, baby. This cherry is mine, and when I pop it, there will be no going back. Ever. You're mine, Elise. Do you understand?"

She licked her lips and nodded.

"Mine. Say it," I commanded.

"Yours," she whispered.

"That's right," I growled. "Fucking mine."

Then I gripped her delicious hips and held her in place as I punched through her thin barrier and sheathed myself completely. "Oh fuck, yeah," I groaned in ecstasy. "You're tight as fuck, baby." I kissed away a tear that had tracked down her cheek and buried my head in her neck as I tried desperately not to move. She was gonna be sore from taking me no matter what, but I didn't want to make it any worse by moving before she was ready. "You okay?" I asked after a minute.

"I think so. I...um...feel really full."

I chuckled and kissed her neck. "Not quite yet. But I promise, when I'm done, you'll be stuffed." I intended to fill her with as much come as possible and hope that my boys did their job fast.

"I...um...can you..."

She trailed off, and I raised my head to gauge her expression, holding back a smile when I saw her blushing furiously. "What do you want, baby? You don't have to be embarrassed with me. You can tell me or ask me anything."

Her inner muscles contracted, and stars danced in front of my eyes for a second. "I think I need you to move," she mumbled.

I rocked against her. "Like that?"

"Yesss," she moaned, pressing her head back into the mattress. "More."

Pulling out a couple of inches, I slowly plush back in. "This much?"

She seemed to realize then that I was teasing because her eyes snapped open and she glared at me. "Harder," she gritted out, one of her hands moving to my chest to lightly tug on my nipple piercing, which I felt all the way in my dick.

I grinned and pulled back just a little, but punched my hips forward this time.

"Yes," she whimpered. "Deeper."

This time, I withdrew almost all the way before slamming back in and holding still. I was shocked at my level of control, but I wanted her to be comfortable with me. Confident that she could ask for what she wanted. And she was cute as fuck when she was irritated. "Like that?"

"Toby," she growled adorably. "Stop teasing me."

"Tell me what you want, Elise," I told her softly.

"I want you to move harder," she murmured, blushing furiously.

"And?"

"Faster."

"You want me to fuck you, baby?" I grunted, punctuating the work "fuck" by bucking my hips.

"Yes!" she yelled. Then she clamped her inner muscles hard, and every last bit of my control shot right out of my body.

"Fuck!!" I shouted as I pounded in and out of her at a furious pace, trying to get even deeper every time I filled her with my dick. "Put your legs around me, baby, and grip that pussy tight around my cock. Oh, fuck, yeah, baby. That's it. Fuck!"

"Toby! Yes! Yes!" Elise wrapped her arms around my torso, burying her face in my neck and pressing her tits against my chest. With every thrust, her diamond-hard nipples scraped over my skin, her nails scored my back, and her moans grew louder. "Yes! Harder, Toby! Oh, yes! Yes! Don't stop! Yes!"

I reached up and grabbed the headboard, then dug my toes into the mattress for more leverage. Some part of me knew I should be taking it easy since it was her first time, but the harder I fucked her, the wilder she became. Her pussy clutched me like a vise, fighting to let me go every time I withdrew.

"Fuck, Elise! Oh, fuck yes! Oh fuck!"

I had no idea how the hell I'd held off my climax this long, but I had reached the end and was about to blow. Slipping one hand between us, I parted her folds with two fingers, then used the middle digit to rub her clit until she shattered, screaming my name at the top of her lungs as her body shook with the force of her orgasm.

Her tight, hot vise grip around my cock sent me spiraling into oblivion after two more thrusts. I buried myself as deep as possible and exploded. Her inner muscles rippled around my dick, milking it so I emptied every last drop of my come inside her unprotected womb.

"Holy shit," I panted as I collapsed on top of Elise, though I was careful not to crush her with my full weight.

"That was..." Her arms and legs flopped onto the mattress bonelessly, making me chuckle.

"Fucking incredible," I supplied.

"Exactly."

She winced when I finally withdrew, and I frowned, silently calling myself twenty kinds of a selfish asshole for taking her so roughly. "Fuck. Shouldn't have ridden you so damn hard. You're gonna be sore as hell tomorrow. I'm not sure you're gonna be able to walk."

Elise turned her head so she was gazing up at me and smiled, her cheeks dusting with pink. "Worth it."

7

ELISE

Waking up to the ache between my legs from giving my virginity to Blade was a heck of a lot nicer than the pain I'd felt from the car crash the previous morning. Those twinges were mostly gone now, but the one in my core from being impaled on my sexy biker's big dick was strong enough that I let out a low groan.

Toby's hold on me tightened, and his scruff scraped against the sensitive skin on my neck as he mumbled, "You okay, baby?"

I nodded, my cheeks filled with heat. "Just a little bit sore."

Gently rolling me onto my back, Toby hovered over me. "Knew I shouldn't have taken you so hard. You were in an accident less than a day ago, and I had to put fucking stitches in your head because of the bastard who ran you off the road. I'm a damn doctor, for fuck's sake."

I lifted my hand to stroke his stubbly cheek. "I was right there with you, urging you on. Asking you to give it to me harder and faster."

"Shh, baby." He dipped his head to brush his lips against mine. "If you keep that up, I'm gonna need to take you again, and you're nowhere ready to have my cock again so soon."

I pressed my thighs together to ease the tingle his words caused. "Then you should stop talking like that before I start begging you to take me again right now. I might be new to all of this, but you've already got me addicted to your dick."

"Damn straight you're new to all this," he growled before claiming my mouth, his tongue sweeping inside to tangle with mine when my lips parted on a gasp. I was breathless and clutching at his shoulders when he finally lifted his head again. "Because you're all mine."

I enjoyed his possessive talk more than I probably should have, considering how new things were between us. "Seriously, if we're not going to have sex anytime soon, you should probably back off before I do something desperate, like hump your leg."

"I didn't say I couldn't get you off, baby." He smirked down at me. "Just that your pussy isn't ready to take my dick again yet."

Even with everything he'd done to my body last night, my cheeks filled with heat, and I dropped my gaze. "Umm..."

"Give me your eyes, baby." He pressed his finger under my chin, tilting my head until I met his steely gaze. "There will never be any reason for you to be embarrassed about something that happens between us. And sure as fuck not when we're in bed together. Okay?"

"Yeah," I whispered.

"Now, do you need me to make you come before we get up to head downstairs to grab breakfast?" He swiped his thumb across my bottom lip. "I'd love to be able to say that I could take my time with you again, but that's not possible this morning. I told Deviant that I'd take a look at an injury he got last week, and he's supposed to meet me in the clinic in fifteen minutes."

"I can wait until later." I nipped at his thumb and suggested, "Maybe you can give me a thorough exam tonight to see if I've healed from your monster dick by then."

He groaned, dropping his head against my chest

and nipping at the underside of my breast. "Fucking hell, I'm gonna have my hands full with you, aren't I?"

"Yup," I confirmed with a grin.

Sliding off the mattress, he tugged me with him, giving my butt a light swat. "Then we'd better get moving so I have enough time for at least one cup of coffee. Gonna need the caffeine to keep me on my toes around you."

Giggling as I got ready, I felt lighter than I had in years. But my good humor dried up when Toby stopped me at the door, his gray eyes serious as he shook his head and said, "You can't go out there like that."

My brows drew together as I glanced down at the jeans and long-sleeved T-shirt I wore. "What's wrong with my outfit?"

"It's missing one thing." He shrugged off his leather vest and slipped my arms into the too-large holes. "You need to wear my cut when we're not in our room so the guys know you belong to me."

For such a short statement, he'd said so much. He'd called his room ours even though we'd only spent one night together. He repeated the thing about me belonging to him...without his dick being inside me. And he wanted me to wear his cut, which was a huge thing if television motorcycle clubs were anything to go by.

My heart raced as I licked my suddenly dry lips. "I can do that."

"That's my good girl." His gray eyes filled with approval as he fisted the leather to pull me close and laid a deep kiss on me. "Keep it up, and you'll earn a sweet reward later."

I licked the taste of him from my lips. "Mmm, sounds delicious."

"It will be." He interlaced our fingers and tugged me into the hallway, locking the door behind us. "For me since I'm not talking about candy."

That was all of the incentive I needed to be on my best behavior. Not that I'd planned to act like a brat anyway when I'd already promised Gideon that I'd listen to his club brothers.

Toby led me downstairs to the kitchen. I spotted the club president's wife making breakfast and decided it was the perfect chance to figure out how I could help around here. And maybe even earn a little extra cash since I wouldn't be working at the bar before I headed back to school. Which I wasn't looking forward to much now that I'd met Toby.

"Hey, Molly." When she looked up to smile at me, I asked, "By any chance, do you need some help with cooking or cleaning? If I'm going to be stuck here until stuff gets resolved, you might as well take advantage of having an extra set of hands around here."

"I'm already pretty much done with breakfast, and one of the prospects will clean up once everyone is finished eating." She tapped her finger against her chin. "But if you need something to keep you occupied and want to earn a little extra cash since you're not able to work at Midnight Rebel anymore, I might be able to find some stuff for you to do at Iron Inkworks."

I'd gotten along well with Molly when we met on Christmas, but her offer and thoughtfulness made me like her more. "That would be amazing. Thank you."

"Thanks for looking out for Elise, but that won't be necessary."

Molly's eyes showed a mischievous glint as she smiled at Toby. "Oh, really? How come?"

"Because she can help me with plenty of shit in the clinic instead. And we won't need to worry about outsiders getting a look at her while she's there since it's on the compound and not open to the public."

"Hmm, yes. Good point." She winked at me.

"I'm sure that's the only reason you want to keep her all to yourself."

Toby tugged me over to the coffee pot and poured us each a travel mug, waiting while I added cream and sugar to mine before leading me to the door again.

"Hey, Blade," Molly called as we left the kitchen.

Toby glanced over his shoulder. "Yeah?"

"Maybe you should have her start by doing an inventory of all those tests you have to keep in stock because your club brothers keep falling like flies. Looks like you were wrong about it being contagious."

Toby heaved a deep sigh, shaking his head as her laughter trailed after us while we made our way out back. When we walked into the clinic, Deviant was already waiting for him, so I waited until he'd replaced the bandage on his arm and we were alone again to ask the question that'd been on my tongue since Molly had teased him.

"What tests was Molly talking about?" My nose wrinkled. "Please don't say that they're STD panels because that would be gross."

"Not even close," he reassured me with a shake of his head. "As ridiculous as it sounds since the

clinic was set up for me to take care of my club brothers, they're actually pregnancy tests."

"Ohh." I giggled.

"Yeah, and I spouted off a bunch of bullshit
when Molly needed to take one not too long ago, so
I'm sure she's enjoying the hell out of seeing how I
am with you." He brushed his lips against mine. "But
she was right about one thing, I could use your help
doing an inventory of all my supplies if you're up
for it."

I rubbed my palms together. "Give me a laptop
to make a spreadsheet, and I'll be more than ready."

I kept busy while I spent the day with Toby at
the clinic, but I still got a lot of insight into the man I
was quickly falling for. He was smart and compas-
sionate—great qualities in a doctor...and boyfriend—
but he didn't take shit from his club brothers. And he
liked to spoil me. From the latte, protein box, and
cookie he had a prospect run out to get me in the
middle of the day to the wad of cash he'd just shoved
into my hand.

"What's this?"

"Your pay for the day."

Shaking my head, I peeled a few bills off and
tried to hand him the rest. "C'mon, it's way too much
for one day's work."

"I hate taking inventory of shit. Don't have to do it at the hospital and come up with excuses to put it off here." He tucked the roll of cash into my back pocket. "As far as I'm concerned, what you did today was invaluable."

"It really wasn't that big of a deal," I denied.

He gave me a kiss that stole my breath and then murmured, "Quit arguing and come up to our room so I can give you your reward for being such a good girl today."

"When you put it like that...who am I to argue?"

8

BLADE

"Chill, Blade," Dahlia sighed and rolled her eyes. "She's safe on the compound, and no one here will touch her while she's wearing your cut."

I frowned, still not convinced that I should go to work and leave Elise. I'd had another day off from the hospital yesterday and having her help in the clinic here the day before meant that I'd gotten way ahead on my to-do list, so we'd spent it cosseted in our room, mostly talking and getting to know each other, and leaving only to get food, then returning to our private little bubble. Everything I learned about her just made me even more certain that she was meant for me. She'd been pretty sore, so I'd told her no sex until she'd recovered. The little minx kept trying to tempt me, so I got creative with ways to make her come, but later that night, she'd woken me up by climbing on top of me and dropping down onto my cock.

Even though I'd lectured myself to be gentle, Elise tended to smash my control to smithereens. She'd bounced on my dick, squeezing her pussy and cupping her big tits, holding them up like an offering. I'd knifed up and latched onto one rigid peak while gripping her hips and lifting her up before slamming her back down.

Afterward, I'd let her recover, then turned her onto her stomach and spanked her ass for disobeying me. However, that had made her so fucking wet that I couldn't resist pulling up her hips and fucking her from behind.

Unfortunately, I was due back to work today and was scheduled for a twelve-hour shift in the ER at Old Bridge General. That was too damn long to be away from my woman when we hadn't found the bastard who'd hurt her yet.

Elise stood from the couch where she'd lounged beside Dahlia and slipped her arms around my waist. "I'll be fine. Your patients need you." She kissed my jaw sweetly, and I sighed, burying my face in her hair. She smelled like fresh, crisp apples, and I was completely addicted to her scent.

"Don't like leaving you when you're in danger," I grunted.

"Am I really, though?"

I raised my head at her exasperated tone and glared at her.

"Is there anywhere safer for me to be than locked up on the compound, surrounded by your brothers, who you know will protect me as fiercely as you would?"

I wanted to argue that the compound had been breached before, but it was a thin excuse since they'd only made it just past the gate. "No," I grumbled.

"Go to work. Save lives like the sexy hero you are, and I'll be waiting when you get back."

"Sexy, huh?" I asked with a grin.

Elise winked and murmured, "So sexy I'm gonna let you give me a very thorough physical when you get back."

Laughing, I hugged her close before kissing her on the forehead, barely suppressing the urge to tell her I loved her. I wasn't sure if she was ready to hear that yet.

"Blade."

I glanced up to see Fox walking into the room. "Got a few minutes before you take off?"

After glancing at my watch, I nodded. "Ten," I told him.

He jerked his chin up in acknowledgment, then turned his focus on his wife as he stopped in front of her. Bending low, he rubbed her protruding belly and whispered something in her ear that made her blush. Then he kissed her before standing and glancing over at me. "Let's go."

"Any news?" I asked as we headed to his office.

"Deviant found the fucker's car in a body shop one town over. Sent Racer and Hawk to check it out. Shop didn't have any info on the seller because they bought it for parts, no questions asked."

"Dammit," I snarled, furious that we'd hit another dead end.

"Don't lose your shit just yet," Fox grunted as we entered the room. He rounded his desk and sat while I stood in front of it, arms crossed and feet braced wide.

"You tell him, yet?" Whiskey asked as he strolled in after us.

Fox shook his head, then looked at me again. "One of the employees—Ned, according to his coveralls—was unusually quiet. Doing his best to be invisible, then slipped out the back. Racer said he was pretty sure the guy was on something, so while Hawk talked to the manager, Racer caught up to Ned as he was getting on his bike. Asshole was about to ride while he was high as a fucking kite. For that alone, I had him brought back here to get his ass kicked. Racer knocked him out while they waited for Stone to show up with a van."

A knock on the door caught our attention, and since it was open, Racer ambled inside. "You tell him?"

Fox rolled his eyes. "Ned woke up on the way here and started crying like a little bitch."

"Didn't make much sense," Racer interjected. "Too fucking high. But he mumbled something about his dealer and the car being in an accident."

My brow rose. "You think he's the customer Elise saw?"

Racer shrugged. "Could be. Or it could be a coincidence. Either way, the asshole deserves a beating. That or the withdrawal should get us our answers."

I frowned, again wondering if I should call out to work.

"Go," Fox urged, clearly guessing where my thoughts had been headed. "Ned won't be any good to us until he's sober. Even longer if we have to wait for withdrawal to kick in for him to talk. Being at the hospital will take your mind off shit. And stop you from driving away your woman by hovering."

Scowling, I growled, "I don't hover."

"Bullshit," Racer snorted, and I tossed him a glare. He put his hands up in a surrender pose but shook his head. "That's what Prez and Mav say, but you've seen what happened ever since they knocked up their women."

I couldn't argue with that, and I had to admit that I probably wouldn't be any better when Elise was pregnant.

Annoyed that everyone had more logic for me going to work than I had for staying home, I dropped my arms and grunted, "Call me if he's ready before my shift is over. Or you find out anything else. Or Elise needs me. Or—"

"Go!" all three men shouted.

I stomped out of the office and returned to my woman in the lounge. After giving her a very thorough kiss, I told her to be good, gave her a pat on the ass, and left for work.

OLD BRIDGE WAS A DECENTLY sized town, but it was surrounded by a bunch of smaller ones that didn't have their own hospital, so we serviced a larger area. Which meant the ER was often busy because people in small towns did stupid shit and there was still plenty of crime. Which was why my day went from treating the burned hand of a kid who mishandled a bottle rocket, to performing surgery on an idiot who crashed their car into a train during a drag race, to a grandmother who thought she was having a heart attack that was actually a bad case of gas, to a teenager with a broken nose because he tried to go to second base with his girlfriend. The last emergency of the day was to deliver a healthy baby girl who didn't want to wait for her momma to be taken to the maternity ward.

I was good at compartmentalizing and used to connecting with my patients while remaining rational and emotionally unattached. But there were always days when my armor was a little weak, and the heavy shit that I dealt with weighed me down. Then some days ended like this, with the smiles of two new parents as they thanked me while holding their pink bundle in their arms.

As I walked away, I wondered if our babies would take after me or Elise...fuck, I hoped they took after her. Then again—I glanced back at the new family and grimaced—if we had daughters who looked like Elise...I'd have to buy a bigger gun collection. And figure out how chastity belts worked. Or build them a fucking tower and lock them away because they would not be allowed to date until I was dead.

With my shift finally over, I hurried to change out of my scrubs and into my street clothes. Despite receiving updates all day, I was anxious to check on my girl. When I arrived at the compound, I parked in the small lot out back between the kitchen and my clinic.

Dinner had been over for a couple of hours, so the room was mostly deserted, except for Maverick and Whiskey who were sitting at one of the tables talking and drinking beers.

"Yo," Mav greeted me when he saw me walk in.

I lifted my chin but kept walking past them, intent on finding Elise and bringing her back to the kitchen to sit with me while I had something to eat.

"She's at the clinic," Whiskey called out, halting me in my tracks.

"The clinic?" I asked, confused.

He shrugged. "Said she had some work to do."

I mentally sighed, knowing she was out there

filing and shit because she couldn't just accept that I would take care of her and she didn't need a job.

Wait...she was at the clinic. It was almost nine at night. Dark. I glared at my brothers. "You let her go there alone?" I nearly shouted as I quickly moved toward the back door again.

"Of course not," Maverick growled, making my pulse and footsteps slow. "Hawk is with her."

"Hawk? Shit," I croaked as I broke into a run. He was a smooth motherfucker with a pretty boy face who had women constantly chasing him. Not that any of them were able to catch him. Hawk had been engaged to the love of his life a few years back until she called it off a few weeks before the wedding. He hadn't been on a single date since...he had trust issues, obviously, but I was pretty sure he didn't want to admit that he still wasn't over her.

Logically, I knew he wasn't interested in Elise, and besides that, none of my brothers would make a move on a woman wearing another man's cut, but jealousy didn't give a shit about that.

When I walked inside the clinic, Hawk was lounging on one of the couches reading, and Elise was at the desk typing on the computer. It was as innocent as I'd expected it to be, yet the need to claim Elise rode me hard.

Both had looked up at my entrance, but I focused on Hawk first. "Out," I said through clenched teeth.

He pressed his lips together, a sure sign he was fighting a smile, which only made me want to rip his balls off. He narrowly escaped my wrath by jumping to his feet and leaving with a wave and telling Elise, "See ya."

I sucked in a slow, deep breath, trying to calm the raging beast inside me. Finally, I turned and locked eyes with my woman.

9

ELISE

My ears barely registered the closing of the door to the clinic as it slammed shut behind Hawk. I was too lost in Toby's amazing lips as he lifted me out of the chair, and his mouth crashed over mine. Then he trailed them down my neck as he wrapped my legs around his waist so he could walk over to the door to lock it.

"I've been thinking about the moment I'd be back here, alone with you, all day, baby," he murmured into my sensitive skin, leaving goose bumps where the scruff of his chin scratched against me.

I sighed, leaning my head back to give him better access as his hot breath sent a sensual shiver down my spine. "The day felt so long without you here."

"That's because you're mine, Elise." He shifted his hold on me so I stared into his intense gray eyes. There was a wicked gleam in them as he cupped my ass and lifted me onto the nearest exam table.

I wrapped my legs around him, pulling him closer.

"No one else gets to be between your legs but me, baby, you got that?" he growled, nipping at my ear.

I gasped, answering by sealing my lips over his again.

I might've initiated this kiss, but Toby quickly took control, devouring me as though he couldn't get enough. Not that I minded even a tiny bit when I was just as desperate for him.

By the time he broke our kiss, my lips swollen and cheeks scratchy from his stubble, I didn't have time to breathe. All of the air was whooshed from my lungs as his rough hands went to my clothed pussy, rubbing against my aching core.

"You already ready for me, baby? This wet pussy ready to take my cock again? Or are you too sore? You need my mouth instead?"

"Yes," I managed to gasp.

"Yes to which question, baby?" He brushed his thumb over my clit, and even with my panties and jeans between us, his touch sent a jolt of pleasure through my body. "I'm gonna need you to be clearer if you want me to give you what you're asking for."

"I'm ready to take you again," I gasped, grinding against his hand.

"That's what I was hoping you'd say." His fingers continued their assault on my aching pussy while he rocked his hips forward. "I'm going to fuck you raw, baby. I'm going to make sure when I come inside you that you feel it. I want to see your belly rounded with my baby."

I gasped again at his filthy words. We'd only known each other a few days, but when he said stuff like that, it was so easy to picture our future together. Toby and me, along with a bunch of light brown-haired little boys with gray eyes just like their daddy. A future that very well might happen if we kept having sex without anything between us. Something we really should talk about...but not in the heat of the moment.

He made quick work of stripping me out of my jeans and shirt—and his cut that showed all of his club brothers who I belonged to when he wasn't around to lay claim to me. My panties and bra quickly followed, so I was completely naked on the cold exam table. Yet he still stood there clothed in his jeans and shirt.

"What about you?" I whimpered.

He grinned, sliding down to his knees. "I need to make sure this pussy really is ready for my cock first. Now be a good girl and spread those legs so I can taste you."

"Yes," I sighed, threading my fingers through his thick hair.

Leaning in, he inhaled deeply before nuzzling his face against my sex. "You smell so fucking good, baby. And I know you taste just as sweet."

I didn't have time to respond because he plunged his talented tongue inside me. Every nerve ending I had must have jumped, a coil of electricity springing to life.

He inched closer, using his muscular forearms to spread my legs as he feasted on me like I was his last meal. Every swipe of his tongue sent a new sensation low in my body.

I was close, so darn close to the edge, and he'd barely gotten started. Something that he must've realized because when his eyes met mine, he hooked a finger inside my wet core.

I cried out, my hips jolting forward as if they had a mind of their own. I needed the release. So much.

As though I'd been waiting every single minute while he'd been gone for just this moment.

"I'm going to come," I managed to breathe.

He moaned, adding another finger into my slippery core as he sucked hard on my clit.

That was all it took to send me over the edge, and I cried out, tossing my head back as the orgasm wracked through my body.

When I finally came down from my high, my body still quivered as I watched Toby quickly shuck off his clothes.

His large dick was already hard as a rock, precome shining at the tip.

"Are you ready for me, baby? Ready for me to fuck this tight little pussy?" He gripped my hips, pulling me forward until he plunged inside my wet folds without waiting for me to answer.

I cried out, getting used to the fullness of his length inside me.

He moaned, closing his eyes slightly as he stilled. "Fuck, you're so wet. So tight. So perfect."

Gripping my chin, he pulled me close so I could smell my own arousal on his breath. "So mine."

He kissed me fiercely, plunging his tongue into my mouth so I could taste my own saltiness on him. Then he moved his hips in the same motion as his expert tongue, making me grip hard onto his waist. I moaned against his lips, unable to even move, my body shaking around his as another orgasm quickly built.

His mouth trailed down to my neck, his nostrils flaring as he breathed me in. "That's it, baby. Come on my cock. Show me how much you like the way I fuck you."

Gripping his shoulders, I hung on as he pounded his hips against me, the angle bringing just the right amount of friction to send me soaring over the edge again. Moaning, I was like jelly as my orgasm took hold, and I held Toby so I didn't collapse right there.

"You're so fucking beautiful when you fly apart for me, Elise," he murmured.

"Wanna see it, too." I dug my heels into his butt, urging him deeper. "Lose control for me, Toby. Please."

"It won't take much. I'm already at the last of my control," he warned. "Hold on tight, baby. I need you to take all of me."

His hips moved faster before his entire body stilled against me, and he let out a low groan that vibrated against my chest.

Catching my breath was difficult as I laid my head on his shoulder, spent in the best way possible.

I thought he was done, but instead, he slowly leaned me back on the table, his dick still inside me as he traced the lines of my thighs.

"I don't know if I can go again," I managed to laugh through my heavy breathing.

"I just need to make sure you've got my come in you, baby. Think you can give me one more orgasm? Spread those legs for me?"

I could barely question his words before his cock was out, and he plunged two fingers inside me, rocking at a steady rhythm that had my already frenzied body on high alert.

"That's it, Elise. Come for me again. Open those legs and let my come fill you up."

I met his hooded stare, the lazy grin on his face as his fingers worked my swollen core.

My eyelids fluttered closed as the fire started in my toes, working its way up my belly.

"Eyes on me," he commanded.

Quickly, I looked at his heated stare.

"I want to watch you while you come."

I did as he obeyed, gripping the sides of the exam table as he picked up the pace of his fingers until my body exploded around his thick digits.

"So fucking gorgeous," he murmured, swirling

his fingers to ride out the last of my orgasm before he leaned over and placed a slow kiss on my belly.

"Is it going to be like this every time?" I asked, running my fingers over his hair, too spent to even move my head.

"Like what?" he whispered.

"Amazing."

He laughed, his whiskers tickling my belly. "This is just the start of us, baby. It's only going to get better from here."

We would need to have a serious conversation about what was happening between us. Sooner rather than later if we kept this up. Sometime when my brain wasn't muddled by the mind-blowing orgasms he'd just given me.

10

BLADE

A short, sharp rap on my door woke me the following morning, and I glanced down at Elise, who was sprawled across me. She hadn't stirred, and a smug grin curved my lips. Probably because I'd worn her the fuck out the night before.

I glanced at my cell on the nightstand and frowned when I saw it was just before five. Careful to disturb her as little as possible, I slid out of bed and pulled on a pair of sweatpants. After making sure that Elise was completely covered even though the visitor wouldn't be able to see the bed unless they came into the room, I padded over to answer the door.

Deviant waited in the hall. "Figured you wouldn't see a text for a while, so Prez sent me to let you know we got a location from the mechanic. He's holed up in a stash house in Dentin."

After Elise and I had returned to my room, I'd received a text from Mav letting me know they were ready to interrogate Ned. I'd taken one look at my woman all snuggled up in my bed, naked and smiling at me with invitation, and replied that I was busy. But he knew I would want to be there when they went after the dealer.

"Ready in ten," I told Deviant before going back into my room and quietly shutting the door. I dragged on jeans and a T-shirt, then shrugged on my leather jacket and laced up a pair of motorcycle boots. Then I went to my closet and retrieved my gun safe and holster. We had an armory that belonged to the club—made legal by having them registered to a gun range we owned—but most of us had a personal firearm, and my CZ 75B was like an extension of my arm. After loading and holstering the gun, I returned the case to the top of my closet.

Once I was ready, I gently kissed Elise until she stirred and blinked her pretty eyes as she smiled sleepily up at me. "I have to go, baby. Club business. But I shouldn't be long."

Her pouty lips turned down, and she raised onto her elbows. "Nothing dangerous, right?"

"Not for me," I answered honestly. We were going to a rough area, but no one would mess with an Iron Rogue, let alone five.

"Okay," she replied softly. "Still...be careful."

"Always. Go back to sleep, baby."

I kissed her one more time, then grabbed my keys from the dresser and shoved them in my pocket as I left the room. Fox, Maverick, and Whiskey waited for me on their hogs when I reached the lot where I'd left my bike. Deviant idled in a dark van a few feet away.

"You let Storm know?" I asked Fox as I swung my leg over my motorcycle.

He nodded. "Shit hit the fan—pretty much what we expected. He wasn't happy about it, but he knows he has to let us handle this shit."

"Let's ride." I put on my helmet and started my engine, then followed my brothers to an execution.

WE DIDN'T BOTHER APPROACHING the stash house quietly or parking our rides in a "safe" area. The Iron Rogues were known and feared around here. People had learned the hard way not to cross us. And as long as we didn't flaunt our activities, the local law enforcement often glanced the other way. Particularly when we were doling out justice, like today. And the police rarely ventured into this area anyway unless they were specifically called, which didn't happen often since the residents were criminals or drug users. No one wanted to bring attention to themselves and risk being busted.

Since it was the dead of winter, the sky was still fully dark this early in the morning. Which would make it easier to approach without spooking our prey. Once I dismounted, I unsnapped my holster for easier access to my gun. The others did the same or chose to tuck their piece into the waist of their pants.

"Ned told us that this lowlife had four other deals going down that night," Whiskey murmured. "When he chased Elise, he basically stood his customers up, and word got out that he was unreliable. He's been crashing here while he tries to gain more clients so he can pay back his supplier."

My lips twisted in disgust as I thought about this asshole and the damage he'd done to countless lives. The dealer's rap sheet had included several drug busts, but he'd also been charged with murder. However, the charges were dropped since the body had mysteriously disappeared. The cops had also picked him up for suspicion in several other deaths, but he'd never been charged for those. They would probably breathe a sigh of relief when they found this fucker dead...and he would be found. Because we intended to send a very clear message.

There was an alley behind the dilapidated old house, and Deviant parked the van on the street at the end of it. We approached the house that way, coming up to the back porch where a couple of guys were passed out and a hooker smoking off to the side of the steps. She started to smile, but when she caught sight of our patches, she sighed and stomped away.

"Blade and I will go in and smoke him out," Fox decided. "Whiskey, cover the front. Mav, stay here at the back. If he comes running out, restrain him, gag him, get him in the van, and meet back at The Room."

He was referring to a small building that sat at a spot on our property that was the farthest from any of the businesses, homes, and clubhouse. From the outside, it looked like a boring cinderblock building, easily overlooked. But on the inside, it was very, very different. We called it "The Room" because the name was as dismissive as its exterior. The interior had four rooms, a lounging area of sorts, a cell, an interrogation hold, and a space that had a cache of tools that might be needed to aid us in gaining what we wanted.

It was most often used as a place for interrogation, but in some cases, we already had the information we needed. Then we used The Room for our particular brand of justice. Tonight, this motherfucker was gonna face his maker in that room. But not before I made him wish he'd never been born.

Deviant had sent everyone a picture of the asshole we were hunting, and I glanced at it one more time before tucking away my phone and pulling out my gun. It was dark, and the guy could be blitzed, making him look bloated or more haggard than usual, so we wanted to be sure we recognized certain features. Luckily, Grey—a world-class hacker who also happened to be a Silver Saint—had obtained security footage from a bodega up the street just before midnight. So there was a good chance the dealer still wore the same clothes.

I followed Fox into the house, stepping over bodies, presumably live ones...but you never knew in places like this. A few people stirred, but they were too fucked up to give a shit who we were and what we were doing there, as long as we weren't cops. Even then, I doubted many of them were capable of running.

Fox paused at a door that looked like it led to a kitchen and glanced back at me, then pointed at a door that went to a hallway. I nodded and quietly made my way toward the front of the house. We met by the door, both of us having searched our first-floor area and coming up with nothing. I jerked my head toward the stairs, and he followed silently as I ascended. The first door on the right was slightly ajar, and muffled noises came from inside. I used the barrel of my gun to nudge it open since I had no desire to touch anything in this place.

A small, dirty lamp on a little table beside a twin mattress rested on the floor. I grimaced when I realized the sounds had been a man receiving a blow job from a hooker. When she shifted, I recognized the junkie's clothing and heaved an annoyed sigh. *Fucking great.*

I flipped off the safety on my gun and pointed it at his head before kicking the mattress to get their attention. The man cursed, and the woman shrieked, scrambling backward when she looked up and spotted my weapon.

"What the fuck?" he slurred as he clumsily reached for the half-dressed whore as she took off. "Get back here, bitch. I paid—"

"Shut him up," Fox snarled.

I bent down and punched him in the jaw, choosing a spot that would cause him a fuck ton of pain without breaking the bone. Then I growled, "Put that thing away and get the fuck up, asshole."

He glared at me...although the effect wasn't really there since his eyes were so bloodshot and glassy. Then he tried to say something but ended up groaning in pain.

"I'm not in the mood to carry your sorry ass out of here, but if you don't get on your feet in the next five seconds, I'll put you in even more pain."

The man grunted and glanced around as if looking for an escape. Once again, I sighed, then kicked the side of his knee, dislocating his kneecap.

He tried to scream in pain, but his jaw was too swollen.

"Blade," Fox muttered.

"What?" I asked casually. "I didn't break it."

His voice was slightly amused when he replied, "Save it for The Room. Just get his ass up and let's go."

"You're right. Why waste all the fun here?" I pointed my gun at the man's groin and snarled, "Put it away, or I shoot it off. I'm not carrying you out of here with your pea-sized dick flopping around."

He grunted and quickly tucked his flaccid shaft

into his pants and zipped up. Then he sat up and tried to stand, but he collapsed when he put weight on his injured knee.

"Fucking hell," I grunted. Swinging my gun toward his head, I aimed for a precise spot that I knew would knock him out but not for long. Then I tucked my gun into the holster and hefted the dealer's body over my shoulder. "Let's get the hell out of here. I'm gonna need to shower for an entire day to get his stench off me."

"Could be worse," Fox mused as we headed down the stairs. "At least he didn't piss on himself."

I snorted, then almost gagged from the stench. "I'd have shot him right here and been done with it before I went anywhere near his piss."

"Agreed."

We exited the house, and I stomped all the way to the van, where Deviant waited with the door open. I tossed the fucker inside and slammed the door shut, then took my first real breath since we'd entered the stash house. It didn't help because I was still mired in the asshole's stink.

"Maybe two days."

SICK AND TIRED of waiting for the dealer to wake up, I grabbed a bucket of ice water and strolled into the interrogation hold where he was tied to a chair. I threw the water at him and tossed the bucket to the side. Happily, it had the intended effect, and he woke up sputtering, then groaned in agonizing pain.

While he'd been unconscious, I injected meds into his jaw to take down the swelling. Otherwise, I wouldn't be able to hear him scream. But it was still bruised and had to hurt like a bitch.

I waited for him to calm down, then I moved to stand directly in front of him. I felt my brothers standing at my back, and when the lowlife finally looked up and saw us, what little color was left in him disappeared.

"You know who we are?" I asked.

His gaze dropped to the logoed patch on the front of my vest, then returned to my face, his eyes filled with terror.

"I'll take that as a yes."

"Blade."

I turned when I heard Maverick say my name, and he held out a black leather medical bag that sported a bright red cross on it. "Seriously?" The bag held some of my special "tools," but he'd clearly added the cross to annoy me.

"I thought it was appropriate," he smirked before pivoting and leaving the room.

I turned back to face my "patient," but Fox stepped up beside me before I could say anything. "Do you see what it says under this patch?" he asked the guy, pointing at his own vest where PREZ was stitched under his road name. "By trespassing on Iron Rogue property, flaunting our rules by bringing drugs into our territory, and for just being a fucking asshole in general, you've earned yourself a trip to hell, courtesy of me."

I set the bag on a little table beside the chair and set out my tools while Fox finished his speech.

"Unfortunately for you, the woman you nearly killed is Blade's old lady."

The dealer winced, and I grinned gleefully just to freak him out.

"Yeah, you understand what that means," Fox concluded. "But just to make sure we're truly on the same page. Do you know how he ended up with the road name Blade?"

The prisoner shook his head.

I twirled a scalpel in my hands and smiled again. Sometimes, the skills I'd learned, like patience and distancing myself from the emotions of a situation, came in super handy elsewhere. Like when you were torturing someone. Very handy.

"He's a surgeon. And he likes to cut things. Well, not things...people. He really just likes to cut people."

"It's amazing," I mused as I picked up another very sharp instrument, "how many places you can cut or stab someone to inflict a fuck of a lot of pain but cause very little damage."

Fox chuckled and cuffed the dealer on the head. "Shoulda known better than to fuck with the Iron Rogues, asshole." Then he said to me, "Let us know when you're done, brother. We'll take care of the rest."

A few hours later, my patient's body gave out, and I calmly cleaned my instruments and put them away in the bag before strolling into the lounge where Deviant and Whiskey waited.

"Ready?" Whiskey asked.

I nodded. "Was gonna do it while he was still alive, but I underestimated how ravaged his body was from all the drug use."

He handed me a small branding iron twisted into the shape of the Iron Rogues logo.

Deviant picked up a blowtorch and engulfed the

metal in fire until it was glowing orange. Then I retraced my steps into the other room and approached the body we'd transferred to a gurney before I introduced him to the full spectrum of my fancy tools.

I grabbed the dead man's chin and turned his head so that I could place the red-hot iron on his cheek. His skin sizzled and popped, filling the room with the rank smell of burning flesh. When I was sure that the brand would be completely clear and unmistakable, but before it cooled enough to tear, I removed the rod and handed it to Deviant, who stalked off.

Then Whiskey and I loaded the body into the van so they could drive it back to the stash house. They'd leave him in the stash house as a reminder of what happened to people who fucked with the Iron Rogues. No one in that place was gonna report the murder, but word would spread among the residents that retribution from the club would be harsh.

The Room was also equipped with a bathroom because it wasn't a smart idea to wander around covered in blood...or whatever else ended up on your clothes while "working." Someone had dropped off a bag with fresh clothes for me, so I took a very long, very hot shower. I'd never be able to scrub myself completely clean, but eventually, I felt as clean as I could get. I dressed in the fresh clothes and hopped onto my motorcycle, taking the long way around so that I reentered the compound from the front.

I was beyond ready to see my woman. Now that the threat had been handled, I wanted to take her home. We were going to have a talk about the future and set a wedding date before I spent the next few days working on putting my baby in her belly.

11

ELISE

Although Toby had assured me that I didn't need to worry about the drug dealer hurting me ever again a few days ago, he refused to even consider me going back to work at Midnight Rebel. I assumed the club business he'd gone to take care of in the middle of the night had been connected to that jerk, but I didn't ask any questions I wasn't sure I wanted the answer to.

Since he wanted to take me to what he called my new home and somehow arranged for another doctor to cover his next few shifts at the hospital, I didn't complain. Instead, I fully enjoyed our uninterrupted time together...expecting things to be very different when I left for my spring semester.

There had been a New Year's Eve party at the

clubhouse, but we rang the night in just the two of us. Instead of sharing a kiss at midnight, we celebrated in bed with lots of orgasms. A new tradition I wouldn't mind honoring for the rest of my life.

The following day, we finally left the little bubble we'd created at his apartment and joined everyone at the clubhouse for a big New Year's Day feast, including black-eyed peas for good luck. Although I quickly started to doubt their efficacy when my brother showed up just after we'd finished cleaning up and glared at Toby instead of coming over to give me a hug.

"What the fuck, Blade? I was only gone for a week, and you've got your hands all over Elise, smack dab in the middle of the clubhouse, as though you have the right to touch her." The woman who had walked into the clubhouse with Gideon looked up at him with wide eyes, and he hurriedly added, "I thought I told you to stay away from my sister."

Glaring at my brother, I shook my head. "And I thought we agreed that you'd stay out of my dating life."

Gideon clenched his fists. "I didn't expect my club brother to move in so quickly on my sister when she was vulnerable."

"Really?" Molly snorted. "Haven't you been

paying any attention to what happens when an Iron Rogue falls for his woman?"

"Did you really expect Blade to be that different from Fox or Maverick?" Dahlia added, shaking her head. "Talk about having big brother blinders on."

The president and VP looked amused by their wives' byplay, but that didn't stop them from tugging them to the bar lining the other side of the room.

Gideon dipped his head to the woman's ear and murmured, "Stay here. I'll be right back after I take care of this."

"Okay," she whispered.

He glanced at Viper, who jerked his chin in response to whatever unspoken communication passed between them, and I couldn't help but wonder what kind of club business they'd been handling that had ended up bringing her back to the clubhouse.

I'd never seen my brother with a woman before, so I wasn't sure how he acted around a girlfriend, but I had a feeling she was important to him. Unfortunately, my curiosity needed to wait for a time when the two most important men in my life weren't ready to beat the crap out of each other.

Toby stepped in front of me as Gideon strode toward us. Heaving a deep sigh, I briefly considered using one of my self-defense techniques to knock him to the floor since he wouldn't be expecting me to attack him from behind. But I decided against it since I didn't want to hurt the big lug when he thought he was protecting me. Instead, I simply moved to his side again and slipped my arm around his waist. Then I held on tight when he tried to move me behind him again.

Smiling up at him, I shook my head. "Gideon would never do anything to hurt me."

"But can the same be said for my supposed brother?" Gideon growled.

Toby's body stiffened next to me, and I stroked my hand down his back. "That's bullshit, Storm. You know damn well that I wouldn't hurt Elise."

"I thought I did, but now I'm not so sure. She's fifteen years younger than you and had just been injured when I left only a week ago. You're the one who treated her after that bastard ran her off the road, for fuck's sake," Gideon roared, his pulse throbbing in his temple. "Isn't it part of the oath you took as a doctor that you're not supposed to get involved with a patient?"

"I do a lot of fucking shit for the club that goes against the Hippocratic oath, and I've never heard you complain."

"Yeah, well...sisters are off-limits. She's family, remember?"

"I get that guys think that's a rule, but that never stopped a Silver Saint when he found his old lady," Molly muttered.

Dahlia nodded. "Yeah, Arya, Rylee, and Wendy would've been sorely disappointed if their men hadn't ignored what their brothers said about staying away from them."

Ignoring the peanut gallery, Toby gestured toward the cut that I was wearing. "She's not just your sister, Storm. She's my woman."

"Been gone a whole week, Blade, but she doesn't have your property patch on her. So your claim isn't permanent," my brother disagreed.

I hated that my brother was right. Toby hadn't given me a vest like the ones Molly and Dahlia wore. He hadn't told me he loved me. And we hadn't even talked about what would happen with us when I left for school. I should've brought it up myself, but I was too happy having him all to myself to rock the boat.

"First, you said you'd *only* been gone a week, and now it's a *whole* week. You can't have it both ways," Gideon argued.

Sheila walked in the front door with Tank right behind her and rolled her eyes when she saw how

Gideon and Toby glared at each other. "We're gonna need to come up with a better system for getting these done." Her gaze darted toward the woman watching my brother with worried eyes, and she sighed. "I have a feeling that making things crystal clear even a few days sooner will help prevent situations like this in the future."

She got close enough to toss a plastic bag to Toby. Then she beamed a smile at me. "Get that sad look off your face, girlie. Your brother is gonna know exactly how serious your man is in just a second. That'll settle this little squabble in a jiffy. Without any bloodshed, which is a good thing since Blade is the one who'd have to take care of any injuries, and he doesn't look too happy with Storm right now."

"Because he's acting like an asshole, and I don't want him to ruin this moment for Elise." Turning toward me, he tugged on his cut to pull me close and gave me a quick kiss. Then he dipped his hand into the bag and murmured, "I was hoping you'd want to trade in my cut for this."

My eyes widened when he took out a smaller version of his leather vest with the words "Property of Blade" stitched on the back. "You want me to be your old lady?"

"Not just that." He dropped to a knee in front of

me. "My wife and mother of my children, too. I love you so damn much, Elise. Can't imagine how empty my life would've been if your brother hadn't carried you through those doors so you could steal my heart with just one look."

"Shit, I had no idea Blade could be so damn romantic," Whiskey muttered.

"Take notes for when you find a woman of your own," Molly suggested, making Whiskey grumble under his breath as he shook his head.

Blade glared at them before returning his attention to me. "You want me to pretend as though I'm gonna need an answer, baby? Or should I just slide my ring on your finger and put on your vest? Because you're already mine."

"How about I just tell you yes?" I whispered, holding out my trembling hand so he could put the gorgeous diamond solitaire on my finger. Then I shrugged out of his cut so he could swap it out with the leather vest I never wanted to take off.

"There, now you look even more perfect than you always do." His eyes heated as he used my property patch to pull me against his chest. "Except there's something else you still need to tell me, baby."

"There is?" I blinked up at him, trying to figure

out what he meant until I realized that I hadn't shared my feelings with him yet. "Oh, that."

"Yeah, that," he growled, giving my butt a soft smack. "Now be a good girl and give me those three little words I've been dying to hear from your sweet lips."

My lips curved at the gagging sound my brother made. "I love you, Toby. With everything that I am."

"Thank fuck."

He lowered his head to capture my mouth in a deep kiss. When we came back up for air, everyone offered us their congratulations. Even my brother. Begrudgingly...before disappearing with the woman he'd brought to the clubhouse.

EPILOGUE

BLADE

"**D**ammit!"

I chuckled when I walked into our bedroom and heard my old lady cursing in the bathroom. She was adorable when she swore, although it made her even angrier when I mentioned that opinion. But Elise was sexy as hell when she was all fired up.

She groaned in frustration again, and I decided to find out what upset her so I could fix it.

My heart skipped a beat when I walked into the steamy room and saw my naked, heavily pregnant wife standing in the shower with water cascading over her. It ran down her delicious curves and dripped off her nipples, making my mouth water.

A shampoo bottle was on the ground, and she

was trying to bend over and pick it up, but her swollen belly was in the way.

"Are you just going to stand there ogling me or help?" she snipped.

I licked my lips as my gaze slowly dragged up her body until it rested on her gorgeous face. "Option number three," I growled with a wicked smirk.

Seconds later, I was naked and joining her in the shower. Slipping my arms around her from behind, I cupped her tits—they'd grown even bigger during her pregnancy—and pulled her back against me. "Gonna get you all kinds of dirty, then help you get clean."

Elise moaned and wiggled her ass against my hard cock. "I definitely approve," she panted. At seven months pregnant, her hormones had gone wild. She was horny all the time, and I had zero complaints about keeping her satisfied.

I massaged her sensitive breasts for a few seconds, then twisted and plucked her nipples, making her cry out and slap her hands against the wall in front of her for support. "I love how fucking responsive you are," I rasped before nibbling on her ear.

After a minute, I splayed one of my hands over her belly, the caveman inside me bursting with pride from breeding his woman. I slipped my other hand between her legs and cupped her hot pussy. She was drenched and not just from the shower, so I easily dipped two digits into her channel.

"Toby..." she moaned, undulating her hips, her body begging for more.

"You have no idea how fucking hot it makes me to know you're walking around with the proof of my claim so blatantly obvious."

Elise half chuckled, half moaned as I pumped my fingers in and out. "Because the ring and property patch weren't enough?"

"Nope," I muttered. "I'm tempted to tattoo my name all over your body, anywhere people can see it. Except right here." I smacked her pussy, making her gasp and shudder with pleasure. "This would be just for me. I don't think I could control myself if I saw my name on your pussy every time I ate or fucked it."

"Then you better have Molly teach you how to give me a tattoo," she breathed. "I love it when you lose control."

I grinned and nuzzled her neck. "Maybe I will. But after the baby is born."

Elise huffed. "The doctor said you don't need to be careful, Toby. I need you. I need it fast and hard. Fuck me."

It never failed to send shock waves of lust

through me when my wife asked me to fuck her. Wrapping my hands around her wide hips, I yanked her ass back, then plunged my shaft inside her. "Fuck!" I shouted as her muscles clamped tight around me. "Love this hot, tight pussy. *My* pussy."

"Yours," she agreed, pushing back against me so that I slid in even deeper.

I loved hearing her admit she was mine almost as much as when she told me that she loved me. It brought out my obsessive need to possess her and back up my claim with action.

Moving my hands back to her tits, I manipulated the stiff peaks as I lazily thrust in and out of her. She was so sensitive that I could make her come just by laving attention on them.

"Come, baby," I ordered in a low, husky tone. "I want to fuck this pussy while it's in the throes of orgasm. Then I'm not gonna let you rest before I make you come again. Maybe even a third time before I blow and fill you until you're so full it's dripping down your thighs."

Elise gasped, then screamed as her climax slammed into her. Her muscles tightened and rippled around my shaft, milking me and nearly making me lose it. But I gathered what bits of control I had left and gripped her hips, holding her steady as

I began to thrust, deep, hard, fast. The sound of our slick skin slapping together mixed with our moans and the hum from the shower spray.

"Yes! Yes! Oh, Toby! Right there! Yes!"

She toppled over the edge again, calling my name and dropping her head back against my chest.

I kept up my pace, working her through it but not letting her recover before I glided a hand to her pussy and swirled a finger around her bundle of nerves.

"One more," I demanded.

"Toby," she moaned. "I can't...oh, Toby. You have to stop! I can't!"

"You will," I growled. I pressed the pad of my finger over her clit and rubbed furiously as I doubled my efforts, fucking her with everything I had.

"I can't—Oh, yes! Yes! Don't stop. Yes!"

"Give it to me, baby."

Her channel squeezed my cock in a vise-like grip right before she gave herself over to the ecstasy of another climax. I couldn't hold back anymore, so I planted myself as deep as possible, my tip ramming into her cervix right before I exploded, bellowing her name.

"I love you so fucking much," I muttered when I finally caught my breath.

"I love you, too," she whispered.

I did as I'd said and helped her wash, then shut off the water and stepped out of the shower to grab a couple of towels. After wrapping one around my waist, I put the other around my woman and helped her step out onto the heated floor. I hadn't skipped out on any of the creature comforts my wife had wanted when building our house.

"How about some breakfast, baby?" I suggested as I gently dried her body.

"You better be talking about food and not eating me," she grumbled. "I'm starving."

"Of course food. You'll need your strength for later because another doctor needed to switch shifts so I have the day off."

"As long as you feed me, I'll let you eat me as much as you want," she said with a mock sigh. "I will make that sacrifice for you."

I chuckled and slapped her ass to get her moving, then followed her into the bedroom. "Watch it. Or I'm gonna fill that sassy mouth with something else."

She looked at me over her shoulder, giving me a saucy smile and a wink. "Promise?"

My cock had only barely gone down after the orgasm in the shower, but her words had me standing at full attention again. Her gaze dropped to my cock, and it twitched as a bead of precome formed on the tip.

Elise licked her lips and turned around to sashay over to me, her sexy hips swaying enticingly. "I think I need a snack before breakfast," she purred.

EPILOGUE

ELISE

I t took me almost six years to finish my degree, but that was what happened when your husband kept knocking you up. Even though I switched to online classes after we got engaged, it was difficult to keep up with my schoolwork while pregnant. Especially when I already had a baby to take care of. And definitely when I was pregnant with a toddler and another baby.

No matter how much help Toby gave me, there were only so many hours in the day. Plus, he had his hands full between his ER shifts at the hospital and tending to his club brothers when one of them got injured. But we had plenty of help from our Iron Rogues family—including my brother and his wife.

However, they were just as busy building their family as Toby and I were.

I'd put my foot down after our third had been born. Toby Jr. and Danny were already a handful, and we'd finally gotten a baby girl their daddy could spoil with Emily.

I loved that I never had to worry about my babies experiencing the same loneliness that my childhood had been filled with, but there were times when I wished things weren't quite so hectic in the house we'd built on the Iron Rogues compound. It was only a few hundred yards from the clinic, so Toby was available in the middle of the night if there was an emergency, making it a handy place for all the kids to hang out. They often did, especially after Toby had a giant playground installed because our baby girl kept babbling about wanting a slide to go down right before her third birthday.

Their laughter drifted through my office window as I worked on the schedule for the last two weeks of the month at Midnight Rebel. It was just one of the tasks I'd taken over for the club after I graduated with my bachelor's degree in business administration. I got to put my love of spreadsheets and organization to good use, and Toby's club brothers could hand off tasks they hated to do. It was a complete win-win all around.

Getting to my feet, I looked outside, my lips curving into a soft smile when I saw Toby pushing Emily on the full bucket swing she'd used for dozens of hours already. Even though the playground had only been finished a few weeks ago, we'd more than gotten our money's worth out of it.

Watching Toby Jr. and Danny race around the perimeter of the soft rubber covering that had been set down on the ground to make sure none of the kids got hurt, my smile widened. They were playing tag with a bunch of their cousins—some who were related by blood and others who were their Iron Rogues family.

It was a beautiful day, and everyone was having a blast, so I decided to leave my work until later and join them. Toby's gaze zeroed in on me as soon as I stepped outside. While I padded across the yard, he bent down to whisper in our baby girl's ear. She was such a daddy's girl, so I wasn't surprised when she tilted her head back and beamed a smile at him. "Otay, Daddy. I be good for Unca Gideon."

My brother took Toby's place behind the swing— Emily had him wrapped around her little finger just as much as her daddy since they only had boys. Then my husband strode toward me.

"I thought you had a couple of hours of work left to do." Pulling me close for a kiss, he asked, "Decided to take a little break?"

Twining my arms around his neck, I beamed a smile up at him. "More like a not-so little one."

"How much time are you talking about?" He wagged his brows at me. "Because your brother owes us for when we babysat his kids last week. I bet we could sneak away while everyone's distracted and put your break to good use."

Going up on my toes, I gave him a quick kiss. "Great, you can help me with a project I decided to start."

His brows drew together as he grumbled, "Damn, I must be losing my touch if you didn't get the sexual innuendo in my suggestion."

"Nope, I didn't miss it." Wrapping my fingers around his wrist, I pressed his palm against my belly. "Having sex is vital to what I have planned. We'll never get the result I have in mind without you filling me up with your come."

His grip on my waist tightened. "Are you trying to tell me that you're ready to give me another baby?"

"Now I'm the one wondering if I'm losing my touch," I teased. "I thought I'd made it kind of obvious."

"Fuck yeah," he breathed, claiming my mouth in another deep kiss that made the kids giggle as they raced past us. I was breathless when he was done, so all I could do was gasp when he tossed me over his shoulder and called out to my brother, "You're in charge for a little while, Storm."

"You gotta be kidding me," Gideon grumbled, his mouth puckering as though he'd tasted something sour. Although Toby and I had been together for years and never hesitated with the public displays of affection in front of him, Gideon still hated any hint of our sex life.

I usually teased him about his reaction, but that was hard to do when I dangled upside down over my husband's shoulder. Then any thought of my brother was wiped from my head when Toby raced upstairs to our bedroom and dumped me on our bed.

Nine and a half months later, we got another baby girl for Toby to spoil. Luckily, Emily loved the idea of being a big sister, so she was willing to share her precious daddy with Lilah.

In the mood for another hero with a piercing...but in a more interesting place? Grab I'm Yours, Baby!

And don't forget to join our newsletter so you don't miss out on news about Storm's release. Plus, we'll send you a FREE ebook copy of The Virgin's Guardian, which was banned on Amazon!

ABOUT THE AUTHOR

The writing duo of Elle Christensen and Rochelle Paige team up under the *USA Today* bestselling Fiona Davenport pen name to bring you sexy, insta-love stories filled with alpha males. If you want a quick & dirty read with a guaranteed happily ever after, then give Fiona Davenport a try!

For all the STEAMY news about Fiona's upcoming releases... sign up for our newsletter!

Printed in Great Britain
by Amazon